seven ghosts

ALSO BY CHRIS PRIESTLEY

The Wickford Doom

Flesh and Blood

Still Water

seven ghosts

CHRIS PRIESTLEY

Barrington Stoke

To Tamsin

First published in 2019 in Great Britain by
Barrington Stoke Ltd
18 Walker Street, Edinburgh, EH3 7LP

www.barringtonstoke.co.uk

A CIP catalogue record for this book is available from the British Library upon request

ISBN: 978-1-78112-894-7

Printed in China by Leo

CONTENTS

Jake heard the clapping and took his headphones off, letting them loop round his neck. He was standing in a group of maybe twenty other children in a large hall lined with mirrors and gold-framed paintings. It was all pretty fancy.

Jake checked his phone and leaned around the boy in front of him to look at the woman speaking. She was standing at the bottom of the huge staircase with polished banisters.

"Good morning, everyone!" she said. "My name is Mrs Fox."

Mrs Fox looked at Jake and seemed to sigh.

"Phones off, please," she told them. "Nothing ruins the atmosphere of a ghost story more than a jokey ring-tone."

Jake muted his phone and put it in his pocket.

"I will be your guide today at Grimstone Hall," she added.

Jake shuffled forward a bit to get a better view. Mrs Fox was a tall woman dressed in smart dark-green clothes. She had pale skin and bright-red lipstick and big glasses with black rims.

Mrs Fox glanced at Jake a second time and gave him another funny kind of look. This made him frown, because who was she to look at him like that? She didn't even know him.

"You have been chosen from hundreds of entrants," Mrs Fox went on as she looked back at the other children. "We felt your stories were the twenty best ghost stories sent to us from schools all across the country. The

Grimstone Hall Trust have been holding this ghost-story competition for several years now. Each year we invite children to submit their stories, and our panel of authors choose the twenty they think are the best. This year they chose your stories. So give yourselves a round of applause."

The group of children paused with embarrassment for a moment, then did as they were asked. Jake joined in, and Mrs Fox clapped too. The children stopped clapping when Mrs Fox did.

"Now on to the business of today," she said with a smile. "As you all know, Grimstone Hall is thought to be the most haunted house in England."

A ripple of excited murmuring went round the group. Jake smiled.

"But there's something more important than that," continued Mrs Fox. "I think we are the only haunted house where all the ghosts

SECURITY NOTICE
HAUNTED
RESTRICTED
AREA
KEEP OUT

are children. It's rather special, don't you think?"

Jake wasn't sure how special it was, but Mrs Fox didn't seem to want an answer to her question.

"I won't overload you with history," Mrs Fox went on. "I will just say that there has been a manor house on this site since the Middle Ages. The house you're in today was mostly built at the end of the seventeenth century by the Gilbert family. A trust bought Grimstone Hall in 2002 with help from National Lottery funding. There had been another plan to make it into flats, but it never happened and the building began to crumble. It was vandalised and burgled. There was a small fire, but we managed to save the building in the nick of time."

Mrs Fox paused to let the children take this in.

"Grimstone Hall became what it is now – a hugely successful hotel, conference centre and venue for writing festivals. It seems there is no shortage of people who want to spend the night in a haunted hotel. People even get married here! An annual horror festival began here in 2005 and has been going ever since. Then the Grimstone Hall Trust decided to have a children's festival too, and as part of that we hold our national ghost-story competition. That's where you come in."

Jake looked at the other children. They all looked just like he thought they would. Nice kids from nice homes. They looked like the kind of kids who couldn't wait to put their hand up in class. The kind of kids who didn't get into trouble. The kind of kids who probably didn't even know what trouble looked like. He was already wishing he hadn't let his English teacher persuade him to enter his story.

"I am going to take you on a tour of the house and some of the grounds," said Mrs Fox. "I'll introduce you to seven ghosts and their stories. The ghosts might even appear to us. You never know."

Two of the younger children at the front gasped.

"I should add," said Mrs Fox. "While many people have seen our ghosts over the years, you would still be very lucky to see one – or, rather, unlucky."

Mrs Fox smiled to herself.

"Afterwards, you will all go back to your schools and write your own story inspired by our day together. The writer of the story chosen as the best will get our lovely trophy and some very generous prizes. So soak up the atmosphere as we go round and see if you can come up with a really wonderful story to wow our judges. Any questions before we begin?"

A girl to Jake's right put her hand up.

"Jasmine, isn't it?" said Mrs Fox, checking her list of names.

"Yes, miss," said Jasmine.

"What would you like to ask?" Mrs Fox went on.

"Have you ever seen a ghost, miss?" Jasmine asked.

A strange look came over Mrs Fox's face, and she paused before saying, "Yes, I have. I have seen all the ghosts at Grimstone Hall."

The children gasped. Jake frowned. Really? It was easy for her to just say that she'd seen a load of ghosts, but did she have proof?

"I will tell you about that later," continued Mrs Fox. "If we have time. Come along. There's a lot to see, and we are having a special lunch in the dining room at twelve thirty. The chef here is rather marvellous but also a bit frightening. He will get very cross with me if we are late."

Someone's hand went up near to Jake.

"Miss," said the boy as he pointed to a mirror on the wall. "Why is this mirror cracked?"

Jake turned to look where the boy was pointing. Jake hadn't spotted the round mirror that looked like a fish eye. It had a thin diagonal crack running across it.

"Ah," said Mrs Fox. "Well, Harry, I'm glad you asked. That is a rather special mirror. It came from a man called Dr Syrus. He was supposed to be a magician. But not the good kind. One of the owners of Grimstone Hall bought the mirror in an auction. He was very keen on objects and books with strange pasts."

"But why is the mirror cracked, miss?" said Jake.

There was something about this mirror that nagged in Jake's mind. Like a memory he just couldn't grab hold of.

"It got broken some years ago," said Mrs Fox. "Before Grimstone Hall was open to the public."

"Isn't breaking a mirror supposed to be bad luck, miss?" said Harry.

"Yes," said Mrs Fox, nodding. "So they say. The mirror was believed to be cursed by Dr Syrus. Some of the trustees of Grimstone Hall wanted to replace the glass, but most felt it might be better to just leave it be ..."

Jake stared at the mirror. Why did it bother him so much? But Mrs Fox clapped her hands as he tried to think, and she started up the staircase. Everyone just watched her go.

"Well, come on," she said, looking back at them. "Follow me. We'll begin with the roof!"

The children set off after Mrs Fox up the grand staircase. Jake followed them but glanced backwards towards the mirror as he went.

When they arrived at the very top of the stairs, the house seemed a bit less grand than it had at the bottom. There were no fancy lights or expensive-looking furniture. The walls were plain and the floors were bare.

"This way," said Mrs Fox, and opened a door to a darker staircase. "Don't be alarmed. This passage is a bit of a tight squeeze and rather steep, but it doesn't last for very long."

They started to climb. Jake was the last one to come out onto the roof.

"Whoah!" Jake said as he stepped out.

"It is rather high up," said Mrs Fox. "Apologies if you suffer from vertigo, but we did ask on the questionnaire you all filled in."

Jake felt dizzy, but he couldn't complain. He hadn't filled in the questionnaire. He couldn't see the point in it. Jake leaned back on one of the chimneys and tried to settle himself. He looked out over the trees and could just make out the top of his block of flats. The tree branches shivered in the breeze and seeing them move made Jake feel even dizzier. Something flapped past his head. Something white and blue. What was that? Jake shook his head. He needed to calm down. He was just freaked out by being this high up, that was all.

“Let’s begin,” said Mrs Fox. “The ghost I am going to tell you about has been seen many times over the years by many people. In 1874, a workman fell from this roof after seeing him. Over a century later, a visiting American general swore he also saw the ghost during an air raid in 1943. But our story starts at the beginning, in 1822 …”

Grimstone Hall had become a very grand house by the end of the eighteenth century. Many of the treasures that still fill the house to this day were collected by Sir Thomas Gilbert in the 1790s as he travelled Europe buying art and antiques.

It was Thomas's son, Sir Clarence, who was master of the house in 1822. After his wife died, Sir Clarence had decided it was time that his son, Henry, learned a bit more about running a large estate like Grimstone Hall.

Sir Clarence was a former soldier. He still had pieces of a French musket ball stuck in his right arm. Sir Clarence had seen terrible things on the battlefield and struggled with the memories of them. He would often fly into a rage. Henry loved his father and feared him in equal measure.

One mild September morning in 1822, Henry and Sir Clarence were riding on their horses along the high lane that ran between two rows of beech trees up on Gibbet Hill. Sir Clarence stopped his horse, and Henry came alongside him as he pointed to the house at the bottom of the hill. The windows glinted in a burst of sunshine when the clouds above them parted for a moment.

"This will all be yours one day, Henry," said his father. "Grimstone Hall and the land that goes with it. You will have a wife and children, and one day you will bring your own son up here and show him this view, just as my father showed me."

Henry nodded and smiled. His father reached over and patted Henry on the back, and they headed off down the hill. They were about halfway down when they saw a small group of people in the road ahead. A boy flying a beautiful blue and white silk kite was running alongside them.

Henry grinned. There had been a picture of a boy flying a kite just like this one in a book his mother used to read to him. It made Henry both happy and sad to see the silk kite in front of his eyes. Happy at the memory but sad that his mother would never read to him again.

"These are travelling folk," said his father. "There's a fair next week at Tunford. I dare say they are heading that way. They will sell things and move on."

The group had come to a halt. They stood in silence watching Henry and his father. The boy had been told to stop flying his kite and stood clutching it to his chest.

"Afternoon, your honour," a man near the front of the group said, and took off his hat. "All the best to you and your boy. All the luck in the world to you."

"I hope I won't find any of my grouse missing," said Henry's father.

"Poaching? Us?" said the man, and his eyes grew wide with surprise. "Not us. There's no poachers here. We don't want your birds. We'll be gone before you know it. No harm done. You have my word as an old soldier of the King, sir."

It was then that Henry noticed the man's right arm ended at his elbow.

"You can stay till Friday," Henry's father told the group. "You may collect any firewood you can find lying around. But then I want you gone. Agreed?"

"Agreed, sir," said the man, saluting.

"That kite," whispered Henry, turning to his father. "I have some pocket money. Can we buy it?"

His father smiled and said, "I say, how much for the kite?"

"Not for sale," said the old woman beside the boy.

"Not for sale?" said Henry's father with a dry laugh. "Don't be ridiculous. Everything is for sale. Just a matter of price. I'll give you a shilling for it – which is a hundred times more than it's worth."

"Not for sale, sir," the old woman said again.

"What does the boy say?" said Henry's father. "Wouldn't you like a nice shiny shilling, lad?"

"He don't talk," said the old woman. "Can't talk. Never has."

"Oh," said Henry's father. "Well, he can nod, I suppose."

The boy did not move except to clutch his kite tighter. Henry's father snorted and pulled his horse away. "Make sure you're gone by Friday," he said. "Come along, Henry."

Henry scowled at the boy and then followed his father. Why wouldn't the boy sell his kite? Those people were poor and they needed the money. It was stupid.

"It's not fair," said Henry as they rode towards the house.

"It is his kite," said his father. "I dare say that boy won't have many things of his own, unlike you."

When they got back to the house, Henry's father told his gamekeeper, Farrow, about the people they'd met. He told Farrow to keep an eye on them and make sure they were gone by Friday. He also reminded Farrow that friends were coming to shoot grouse on Saturday.

*

Henry could not get the kite out of his mind or the feeling of irritation he had with the boy, the old woman and his own father. He felt the three of them had clubbed together to make sure he did not get the kite.

Henry was still sulking when Farrow came running into the courtyard that Saturday.

"Fetch the master!" Farrow shouted.

Someone went to find Henry's father.

"What's the matter, man?" he asked when he arrived.

"There's been an accident," said Farrow. "It's the shooting party up on Gibbet Hill. One of them has ..." Farrow didn't finish his sentence. "Best that you come, sir."

Henry's father followed Farrow, and Henry followed them both across the moor. They stopped by a small group of trees near where Henry and his father had met the old woman and the boy with the kite. Henry could see the boy now, lying on his back in the heather. The front of his shirt and his face were all red with blood.

"He just ran out from behind a tree," said a man nearby, his gun in his hand. "Right into my line of fire."

"Put something over the boy, Farrow," said Henry's father. "See if you can find the boy's people."

Farrow told some men to go and look for them.

"Is he ...?" Henry began to ask, staring towards the boy's crumpled body.

His father nodded. "I'm afraid so, my boy. It's a terrible business."

Henry saw the kite lying on the ground near the body. His father followed his gaze.

"Well, I'll say one thing for you, Henry," said his father. "When you are determined to have something, you don't give in. Go on – you may as well have the kite. The boy has no need of it now, I suppose."

Henry hesitated a moment, then headed towards the kite. Farrow's disapproving look gave Henry a sudden pang of guilt. But Henry wanted the kite. He picked it up and walked away, but after a few steps the kite snagged. Henry turned round and saw the string of the kite leading back to the dead boy. He was still clutching it in his hand. Henry gave it a sharp tug and freed the string, but he felt a cold chill run over him as he walked away, and he did not look back.

*

Henry saw Farrow walking across the courtyard the following day. "Will there be a funeral?" Henry asked him.

"A funeral, Master Henry?" said Farrow without turning round.

"For that boy," said Henry. "The one who … You know …"

"The boy who was shot, Master Henry?" said Farrow. "The boy whose kite you now have?"

Henry didn't like Farrow's tone of voice.

"No, Master Henry," Farrow continued. "There won't be a funeral. Not the kind you're thinking of anyway."

"Why?" said Henry.

"They are travelling folk," said Farrow. "They have their own ways. They took the boy's body and they will deal with him in their own way. Now, if you'll excuse me, Master Henry, I have some work I must attend to."

*

Henry flew the kite as often as he could. He sometimes saw Farrow looking at him when he did, and Henry didn't like it, but it just made him fly the kite even higher. Why should he care what Farrow thought?

Henry often had the feeling he was being watched even when Farrow wasn't about. He slept with the kite beside him on the floor, with the string around his hand. One night he woke and felt the string being tugged. But when Henry looked around, there was no one there. Or so he hoped.

Henry sometimes dreamed of the mute boy walking across the lawn. He'd be looking up at Henry's room, his arms outstretched, begging for the return of his kite. But it was Henry's kite now!

Then one day while Henry was outside flying the kite, a sudden gust of wind yanked it out of Henry's hand. To his horror, it sailed away and got snagged on one of the pinnacles up on the roof.

"Farrow!" cried Henry. "My kite."

"Oh dear," said Farrow. "That is a shame, Master Henry."

Farrow didn't sound as if he thought it was a shame at all, and he laughed when Henry asked him to climb up and get it. Henry complained to his father, but he just laughed as well. Henry did not see what was funny. Tears started to fill his eyes.

"But what about my kite, Father? I want my kite back! It's not—"

"Oh, for goodness sake, Henry!" snapped his father. "Do stop going on about that silly kite. You're too old for this nonsense."

Henry refused to eat his supper and was sent to bed. Cook sneaked a sandwich up to Henry, but he wouldn't even eat that. He didn't sleep very well and woke early.

As soon as he was dressed, Henry went out onto the lawn to see if his kite was there. He hoped that it had come loose in the night and fluttered to the ground somewhere.

A huge grin appeared on Henry's face as he saw the kite. It was no longer snagged on the roof but up in the air fluttering about. Henry followed the string of the kite, which seemed to lead to a place on the parapet of the roof. He knew there was a small door near there.

Henry rushed back inside the house and crept up to the small stairs that led to the roof. He had been banned from coming here years ago, but he was older now. Besides, no one would know, as long as he was quiet.

The sun had risen further, and there was a cold light now as Henry stepped out into a confusing collection of chimneys and pinnacles. Then he saw the kite. Henry grinned and moved forward.

Henry came round one of the chimney stacks and saw a boy standing with his back to him. The kite danced in the air above the boy, flickering in the dawn light.

"Hello," said Henry. "You there."

The boy slowly turned. Henry recognised him, despite the damage done to his face and chest by the shot. Henry staggered backwards, his mind struggling to cope with what he was seeing, and screamed.

*

Henry never really recovered from the shock of seeing the ghost of the boy on the roof. He said he continued to see the boy flying his silk kite from the rooftop. Henry could hear his feet scampering among the chimneys. Sometimes the boy even crept into his bedroom at night, Henry was sure of it. In the end, Henry could not be calmed and was taken to stay with relatives far away. He never returned.

It made Henry's father furious at first. Then it made him sad. Then it broke his spirit. Henry's father had dreamed of handing the estate on to his son, but now he could see that would never be. Some years later he sold Grimstone Hall to Sir Thomas Warner, a man who had made his fortune in – of all things – silk.

"Poor Henry," said Jasmine.

"What about that boy whose kite Henry pinched?" said Jake. "He got shot and died, remember?"

Jasmine didn't reply.

"It's a sad story," said Mrs Fox. "So many ghost stories have a bit of sadness about them. Sadness and cruelty. Maybe think about that when you write your own stories."

Mrs Fox looked straight at Jake, and he had to glance away.

"So," she said, "shall we move along to our next ghost?"

The children followed Mrs Fox back inside the house and downstairs to the second landing. They turned onto a long dark corridor. Mrs Fox stopped outside a door, paused and then opened it.

The children squinted at the bright light bursting out from the room. Mrs Fox went in, her figure black against the brightness, and the children followed. As Jake was going in, he turned to look back down the corridor and thought he saw a girl. A pale, skinny girl. Just for a second. She was wearing an old-fashioned long dress that reached right to the floor, with an apron tied around it. Jake almost called out to tell the others, but then she was gone.

He smiled. The people at Grimstone Hall must think kids were stupid or something. If they wanted them to think this girl was a ghost, they needed to make her look like a ghost. She should float about on a wire or glow or something. Besides, Jake was the only one who saw her, so their little show had been a waste of time.

Jake squeezed into the room to stand at the edge of the group. They were in a bedroom. Much bigger than his bedroom at home and a hell of a lot tidier. Instead of posters on the walls, there were small paintings. One was of a vase of flowers, one a horse in a meadow, another some mountains and a lake. All very sweet – if you liked that sort of thing.

"We call this room the sickroom," Mrs Fox said.

"The sickroom?" said a girl at the front.

"It's just a bedroom, really," said Mrs Fox. "Any room could become a sickroom in a Victorian house. People with money didn't go to hospitals – they were for poor people. If you had money, you got looked after at home. Maybe even by a professional nurse. This room was once occupied by someone who needed looking after because they were old and not very well. She was called Lady Agnes – but the story is really about her young servant girl, Maisie."

Jake looked back at the door, thinking about the girl he had seen in the hallway outside.

"This particular ghost was seen just last week by a young man staying here," Mrs Fox went on. "He was returning to his room late at night, and the ghost ran past him on the stairs. The young man followed her and saw that she was hurrying to this room. When he opened the door, the room was empty. He was delighted, of course. He was one of the many people who come here in the hope of seeing something just like that ..."

One of the girls near Jake rolled her eyes at the weirdness of this idea, and he smiled. What sort of person goes looking for ghosts?

"The story of our second ghost takes place in winter," said Mrs Fox. "It was the beginning of 1872. Queen Victoria had been on the throne for almost thirty-five years, and the Warner family had owned Grimstone Hall for even longer ..."

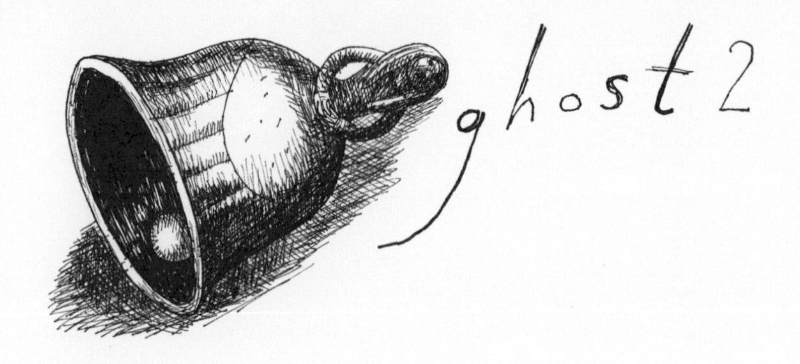

It was a cold and damp February day in 1872, and Maisie and the rest of the servants had gathered on the steps of Grimstone Hall. They were waiting to greet Sir Michael Warner as he returned home from his honeymoon.

None of the staff had met Sir Michael's bride, but they were glad that their master was finally settling down. Sir Michael's father had died the year before, and they had all been worried that Grimstone Hall might be closed down for good.

Sir Michael's carriage rumbled to a halt, and the horses were held and the doors opened. He stepped out, followed by his wife. Then, to everyone's surprise, an older lady also appeared. She turned out to be Sir Michael's elderly mother-in-law, Lady Agnes.

Lady Agnes was dressed all in black, and her slow, jerky movements reminded Maisie of an insect. She seemed very frail and needed to be helped up the steps of the house. As Lady Agnes passed Maisie, she shot out a thin hand and grabbed the poor girl's arm, making her jump.

"You're a pretty little thing, aren't you?" said Lady Agnes as she peered at Maisie from behind her black veil. Maisie wanted to pull her arm away. The old lady scared her.

"Healthy too," said Lady Agnes, raising her bony hand to Maisie's face. "Look at those rosy cheeks."

"Thank you, madam," said Maisie nervously.

Lady Agnes smiled and let go of Maisie's arm. She moved up the steps and into the house, coughing and wheezing. Maisie breathed a huge sigh of relief, and Mrs Miller, the housekeeper, patted her on the back.

"Come on, rosy cheeks," Mrs Miller said. "Work to be done, my girl."

Some of the servants at Grimstone Hall who weren't local got homesick, but not Maisie. The workhouse was the only home she'd known before Grimstone Hall. Anything was better than the workhouse, where they'd been treated worse than animals, worked to the bone for barely enough food to live on and beaten if they complained about it. Mrs Miller was kind and fair, and Maisie was a good worker. She liked to be busy, so she was glad to see the rooms being used again now that Sir Michael was home.

It was warmer too now that there was a fire in every hearth. Maisie was cleaning a fireplace when Mrs Miller called her name. It made Maisie jump up and bang her head on the mantlepiece.

"What is it, Mrs Miller?" said Maisie, rubbing her head.

"It's Lady Agnes," said Mrs Miller. "She's asking for you."

"Me?" said Maisie.

"You must have made an impression with those rosy cheeks of yours," said Mrs Miller.

Maisie grinned at the joke. "What does Lady Agnes want?" she asked.

"Well, I suppose you'd better run along and find out," said Mrs Miller. "Go on – off you go. I'll finish that fireplace."

Maisie dusted her hands on her apron and headed up the stairs to Lady Agnes's room. She knocked on the door, and a shout from the other side made her jump.

"Come in! Come in!"

The voice was so harsh, Maisie thought. But she opened the door and let herself in.

Lady Agnes was in bed over by the window, but the shutters were closed. It took Maisie a few moments to get used to the dark.

"Well, don't just stand there," said Lady Agnes. "Let's have a proper look at you."

Maisie walked over towards the bed.

"Now then," said Lady Agnes. "It's Maisie, isn't it?"

"Yes, madam," said Maisie.

"Well, Maisie, you are to look after me," Lady Agnes told her. "What do you say to that?"

Maisie didn't know what to say. Lady Agnes chuckled.

"You don't seem very pleased," said Lady Agnes.

"Sorry, madam," said Maisie. "I just ... That is, I don't ..."

Lady Agnes waved her hand and frowned. "Shhh," she said. "You are to come when I call, do you understand?"

"Yes, madam," said Maisie.

"Just you," said Lady Agnes. "Only you. Come whenever I call. Do you understand?"

She reached out and grabbed Maisie's hand.

"Yes, madam," said Maisie.

"Good," said Lady Agnes after a moment. She let go of Maisie and lay back against her pillows.

"Can you reach the bell pull, madam?" said Maisie. "I can move the bed a bit—"

"No, no," said Lady Agnes. "I have my own bell."

"Madam?" said Maisie.

Lady Agnes reached under the covers and brought out a small brass bell. Then she motioned for Maisie to come closer.

"Pretty, isn't it?" said Lady Agnes.

Maisie wasn't at all sure it was pretty. It was an odd thing. It was brass and in the shape of a servant girl, with a bonnet and an apron. The body was the handle and the dress was the bell.

"It looks a bit like you, doesn't it?" said Lady Agnes. She smiled and a shiver ran over Maisie.

"When I ring this bell, you are to come at once," said Lady Agnes. "Do you understand?"

"Yes, madam."

"At once," repeated Lady Agnes. "Whatever else you're doing."

"Yes, madam," said Maisie.

"Well, don't just stand there," said Lady Agnes. "Get on about your work, you silly girl."

Maisie bowed and scurried away. She waited until she reached the bottom of the stairs and then let out a sob, clamping her hand over her mouth to muffle the sobs that followed.

"Maisie?" said a voice behind her.

She turned to find Mrs Miller standing in the doorway.

"I can remember when I was your age," said Mrs Miller. "Away from home. Away from my parents ..."

"My parents are dead, Mrs Miller," said Maisie.

"I know, my dear," she replied. "I'm sorry. But we're your family now. We'll look after you. Lady Agnes is an old woman. She's ill. Maybe she just wants for a bit of kindness."

There was the sound of a bell, and Maisie looked up the stairs.

"Well, off you go, girl," said Mrs Miller.

Maisie nodded and set off up the stairs. She knocked at Lady Agnes's door.

"Come in!" called Lady Agnes.

Maisie opened the door and stood with her hands clasped behind her.

"What took you so long?" said Lady Agnes.

"I came as fast as I could, madam," said Maisie.

"Do not answer back," said Lady Agnes.

"Sorry, madam."

"Get me some tea," said Lady Agnes.

"Yes, madam."

*

Lady Agnes worked and worked Maisie. She rang her bell all hours of the day. She rang it during the night as well, but no one apart from Maisie was disturbed by it. The sound of the bell seemed to carry through walls and doors and seek only Maisie out. The rest of the household slept on, but Maisie was forced to leap out of bed and scurry away in the darkness to see what Lady Agnes wanted.

Maisie became paler and paler. Whether it was down to tiredness or some chill caught while running about the halls at night, no one could say. Her eyes started to lose all their previous sparkle.

She became so ill that she was forced to take to her bed for a couple of days. But as soon as Maisie could stand, Lady Agnes was ringing her bell again and Maisie was set to work once more.

Mrs Miller brought the matter up with Sir Michael, but he didn't want to listen and handed it over to his wife. She sharply reminded Mrs Miller of her place and that her mother was ill and might die any day, so she should show some compassion.

Maisie struggled on. Mrs Miller complained again and was sacked. The servants gathered tearfully on the steps of the house to watch Mrs Miller leave. They were devastated. Mrs Miller was like a mother to the girls who worked there, and none more so than Maisie. She was a shadow now of the girl she had been before Lady Agnes had arrived.

On the other hand, Lady Agnes grew stronger and stronger each day. Not that it stopped her ringing the bell. It was as if she wanted to squeeze every last drop of life out of Maisie. The word "witch" was whispered on the servants' stairs and in the kitchen.

Maisie collapsed at the bottom of the stairs one day. By the time she was found, the poor girl was dead. Mr Norris, the butler, said later that picking Maisie up was like picking up a handful of leaves, she was so light.

Mr Norris tried to explain to Sir Michael some of the bad feeling about what had happened to Maisie, but he would not listen. Sir Michael grew angry when Mr Norris would not let the subject go. It was clear to Mr Norris that he would end up being sacked like Mrs Miller if he carried on, and so the matter was dropped.

Maisie was buried in the local churchyard. Sir Michael did pay for a headstone at least.

*

Lady Agnes was now well enough to take a short walk in the garden with her daughter when the weather allowed it. She would also join the others for dinner and play cards on the rare occasions there were guests.

The servants were all wary of Lady Agnes, but no more was seen of her bell. And many of the servants had left after Mrs Miller was sacked. A new factory had opened in the local town, and the pay there was better. The new staff brought in to Grimstone Hall did not believe those who swore they had seen Maisie worked to death.

Betty, one of these new maids, was putting clothes away in Lady Agnes's chest of drawers when she saw the bell. She took it out and shook it, smiling at the loudness of its ringing.

"No!" shouted Lady Agnes, coming back into the room and snatching it from Betty. "You stupid girl!"

Betty scurried away, and Lady Agnes stood by the window. She was about to go back downstairs when something caught her eye in the twilight outside. Standing on the lawn, looking up at the window, was Maisie.

"No," said Lady Agnes, closing her eyes and shaking her head. "No, no, no ..."

When Lady Agnes opened her eyes and looked back at the lawn, it was empty. She smiled to herself and wrapped the bell in linen, making sure to stuff the linen inside the bell

2
2
2
2

so that it would be completely muffled. Then she put the bell in a wooden box beside her bed, locked it and put the key in the pocket of her dress.

Lady Agnes fell into a deep sleep. She was woken by the sound of a bell. At first she thought it was church bells ringing a long way off. She remembered how she used to lie in bed when she was a girl and hear the bells ringing in the village down the lane.

But the tone of the ringing changed. It became more harsh. It couldn't be. It sounded like the bell she had bought from the old tinker woman. The bell in the shape of a servant girl. The bell the tinker had promised would make her well again. The one bell she had rung for that silly girl. The one who ...

"Yes, madam," said a familiar voice.

Lady Agnes tried to adjust her eyes to the gloom.

"Who's there?" Lady Agnes demanded. "Show yourself!"

"Yes, madam?" said Maisie, her voice sounding dry and distant. "I came as fast as I could."

Maisie walked slowly forward out of the shadows. Her face and clothes were flecked with graveyard soil. Lady Agnes screamed and woke the whole household.

It took some time for anyone to get any sense out of Lady Agnes, and the story she told between gasps and sobs made no sense at all. She raved about a bell and the poor servant girl who had recently died. Two days later, Lady Agnes breathed her last breath.

Her daughter thought it wise to bury the strange bell with Lady Agnes.

Mrs Fox waited for the story to sink in as the children stared at the empty bed. Jake thought about nasty old Lady Agnes and her bell. The girl he'd seen in the corridor was clearly meant to be poor Maisie. That was pretty cool actually. Kind of creepy in a way. Just having her wander around like that and not making a big deal of it.

Jake wondered if there were going to be any more of these shows. Maybe that was what the guy who was staying here saw the other night. Maybe the hotel hired a whole team of these "ghosts" just to please the weirdos who came here for a glimpse of something.

"Come on," said Mrs Fox, with a clap of her hands. "I think we all need a breath of fresh air!"

Jake followed everyone out of the sickroom. The group headed downstairs after Mrs Fox and then past the kitchens and right out of the house.

"Please keep to the paths," said Mrs Fox without turning round.

They went down a brick path via a gate in a high wall, then down some worn and cracked stone steps. They came to a halt in front of a strange small domed building set into the lawn they'd just walked past. The building was almost completely overgrown by ivy and stood in the shade of a group of trees. The heavy wooden doors were locked with a padlock. It felt cold and damp out. The girl in front of Jake hugged herself and rubbed her arms.

"Does anyone know what this is?" asked Mrs Fox, pointing to the building.

A boy put his hand up and said, "Is it an igloo, miss?"

There was a ripple of giggles from the other children, and the boy blushed.

"No," said Mrs Fox. "But good for you for having a go. It just so happens you're nearer to the truth than you might think. This is an ice house. Not a building made of ice, but a building to store ice. Back in the old days – before electricity or fridges – they had to store ice in cold places such as this. They would bring the ice here and shut it away, and it would last for months. Ice for drinks made without any electricity at all. Amazing when you think about it."

A girl next to Jake wrinkled her nose. "But ice from a revolting old cave," she said.

Jake smiled. *A revolting old cave?* Who talked like that? He wondered what kind of school this girl went to. Not one like his, that was for sure.

"Yes," said Mrs Fox. "You have a point. Anyway, this ice house is the chilly setting for the story of our next ghost – a ghost called the Frozen Boy."

It was December 1893 and Queen Victoria was still on the throne, but Grimstone Hall was now owned by the Harrison family. Sir Herbert Harrison was a wealthy man, having made his money in steel. He was an important adviser to the government. The Prime Minister, Mr Gladstone, had come to dinner at Grimstone Hall twice.

Sir Herbert was always keen to take any chance to look like a man of the people, so he opened the gates of Grimstone Hall to the local villagers every Christmas. A lot of the servants had family in the village, and for the few hours that they visited, the house had a warm glow. It was a contrast to the normally rather chilly atmosphere of the place. Sir Herbert was a busy man and found family life a rather bothersome distraction.

But Rupert couldn't stand his father's fake smile and the fake voice he used when talking to the villagers. It was all fake. All of it. Rupert hated the invasion of children from the village into his home. His father expected Rupert to entertain them. But what was he supposed to do? Rupert wasn't going to pretend to like these children – and they weren't going to pretend to like him.

Rupert watched them running about, stuffing their faces with food. Yet his father always told him that he ate too much and made too much noise when he was eating. In fact, the only times Rupert's father seemed to notice Rupert were when he was doing something wrong. Or something his father felt was wrong.

Rupert's mother was just as bad. She sang the carols far too loudly. It was embarrassing. Rupert's mother never sang otherwise. Ever.

And for good reason. He could see the servants trying not to laugh at her.

Rupert could stand no more and went outside. The sound of carols seeped out from the dining hall as Rupert stomped across the garden. He couldn't wait to get back to school.

The snow that Rupert had hoped for had never arrived. Christmas wasn't the same without snow and snowball fights and sledging on the hill above the house. But this year, it wasn't even that cold. The only ice Rupert had seen was in the bucket one of the servants was now carrying back from the ice house.

Rupert noticed that some of the village children had gathered together and were playing hide-and-seek. He felt suddenly guilty that he hadn't made more of an effort with them. It might be fun to play hide-and-seek in the grounds. Especially at night.

But Rupert knew he could not join in. They would never let him. He might hide all night and no one would come to find him.

Rupert noticed that the servant had left the door of the ice house open. His father would be furious at the servant when Rupert told him. Just as he was thinking this, one of the village boys ducked into the ice house to hide. Rupert smiled. Thes boy clearly had no idea what the ice house was, or he would never have gone in there.

The thought of closing the door came to Rupert almost randomly. He strode over to the ice house and shoved the heavy door shut. The boy inside called out, but the door was so thick and heavy that it was hard for Rupert to hear him even when he was standing next to it.

Rupert walked away, chuckling, and went back inside the house. He picked up a mince pie and bit into it as he watched his mother sing "Hark! The Herald Angels Sing" at the top of her voice.

*

No one found the boy until much later, when the boy's mother came to the house saying he hadn't arrived home. Sir Herbert was not at all pleased to be dealing with this at nearly midnight but sent men out to search the house and grounds.

They found the boy in the ice house. Cold and dead. Rupert had been in bed asleep but was woken by the commotion. He came down the stairs as they brought the boy into the house. The boy's mother screamed out and collapsed to the floor. Rupert saw the boy's face. It was pale like marble. Almost blue.

"Go back to bed, Rupert," said his mother.

"But what's happening?" Rupert asked.

"There's been a frightful accident," she replied. "Go back to bed and we'll talk about it tomorrow."

But Rupert couldn't sleep. Shouldn't he say something? Perhaps he should go downstairs right that minute and explain. He had forgotten all about the boy in the ice house. He had assumed the boy's friends would find him and free him.

Yet what good would it do to tell anyone? It wasn't as if Rupert had meant the boy to die. It's not as if he had locked him in. The door was heavy. It must have jammed. But that was hardly Rupert's fault, was it?

Rupert's mother was too upset to come down to breakfast the following morning. Sir Herbert was clearly furious at the effect this might have on his popularity when the story got out in the newspapers. It was a disaster.

Rupert was mostly ignored as usual. No one seemed to suspect he was involved. He did have the odd pang of guilt but reminded himself again that he really was not to blame.

Then the servant Rupert had seen collecting ice came forward and admitted to Sir Herbert that he could not be entirely sure he had closed the door of the ice house. He was dismissed immediately and was told to leave the estate at once. It seemed as if that was that.

All Rupert had to do was get through the next few days and then he would be back at school with his friends. It wasn't long now. Perhaps it would snow while he was at school. That would be more fun anyway.

Rupert walked across the lawn, thinking about what fun it would be to have a huge snowball fight in the school grounds. He was in such a world of his own that he did not notice the boy at first.

But when Rupert looked up, he stopped, horrified, as he saw the boy from the ice house walking towards him in the moonlight. It was impossible. Yet there he was. The ground the boy stepped on froze instantly and sent sparkles of frost across the grass towards Rupert's feet.

The boy was a terrible sight. His skin was almost glowing, with a pale-blue tinge to it.

3
3
3
3

There was frost around his lips and around his eyes. They twinkled in the twilight.

"No!" cried Rupert. "It can't be! It can't be!"

Rupert turned to run, but the damp grass was now frost beneath his feet, and he slipped and fell. Before he had time to scrabble to his feet, the boy was standing over Rupert, reaching out his cold blue hand.

*

They found Rupert curled up on the damp grass. The servants who came when they heard him crying were puzzled by the frost on the grass – the day had been so mild, and there was no sign of frost elsewhere.

Rupert was shivering – cold to the touch. The servants carried him inside and built up a fire, but it seemed no amount of heat would warm him. Rupert's mother took him to stay with friends in the South of France.

But Rupert never felt warm again for as long as he lived, and he refused to return to Grimstone Hall. The ice house was locked and has never been opened since.

The boy next to Jake shivered. It did seem to have got colder by a few degrees. They all looked at the padlocked door to the ice house. Mrs Fox rubbed her hands together.

"We don't know the name of the Frozen Boy," said Mrs Fox. "But he has been seen many times over the years. Shall we press on? If you'll just walk with me over to the terrace."

When they moved away from the ice house, Jake noticed that the boy standing next to him did not move. He turned to tell the boy to come on, but he was gone.

Jake stood there for a moment, staring at where the boy should have been, then shook his head and went to catch up with the others.

The children followed Mrs Fox onto the terrace. It ran alongside the house and faced a lake, some woods and a small hill with what looked like the ruin of a castle on top. Mrs Fox stopped by a sundial, and the children gathered round. Jake put his hand up. Mrs Fox smiled at him.

"Is that a castle, miss?" Jake asked.

"The tower you see on the hill over there isn't the leftover ruins of a castle," she said. "It isn't really even a ruin. A ruin is something that was once a building but has partly been destroyed. The tower was built that way."

"What do you mean?" Jake said.

"The grounds of Grimstone Hall were landscaped in the eighteenth century. It was the fashion then to build fake ruins and towers to make the view look more like a painting. They are sometimes called follies – or eye-catchers. Because they were there to catch your eye, you see. To be a point of interest in the landscape. But there's no need for us to plod our way over there. It looks like it might rain. Let's go inside where it's a bit warmer, and I'll tell you about the next ghost."

Once inside, Mrs Fox turned her back to the children and looked out of the window towards the tower.

"This ghost is one that witnesses seem to be particularly alarmed by," said Mrs Fox. "This might be because he is always seen in daylight, among the trees over by the lake, when people are taking an otherwise peaceful stroll. It is scary to glimpse something in the darkness and shadows but worse to see something out in the open, as clear as day, and know that there can be no mistake."

Jake nodded. She had a point.

"The story of this ghost," Mrs Fox went on, "brings us into the twentieth century ..."

ghost 4

The Harrison family sold Grimstone Hall to an American millionaire, but he never lived in the house. Instead, just a small band of servants looked after it. Most of the rooms were closed down, the windows shuttered and the furniture hidden under dust sheets.

By the summer of 1911, Grimstone Hall had been sold again. It became the family home of Sir Andrew Carter, his wife, Lady Emma, and their eight-year-old son, William.

William had been a sickly boy and almost died when he was very young. He was small for his age and very slight. Lady Emma had been told she might not have any more children and was very protective of William.

Sir Andrew found this very irritating. He felt that William needed to be encouraged to get out and play, not sit indoors all day reading and drawing pictures.

Lady Emma refused to send her son away to school. A private tutor was hired, but the tutor seemed as over-protective of William as his wife. All Sir Andrew heard about was how sensitive William was. How imaginative. Sir Andrew blamed this sensitivity on his wife. She was forever claiming to see spirits in the house and grounds – a boy with a kite on the roof, a servant girl who ran around the house at night. Sir Andrew found such nonsense very tiresome.

Boys were not meant to be imaginative as far as Sir Andrew was concerned. Certainly not sensitive! Sir Andrew was determined that no son of his was going to end up as a poet or a painter or some such.

An idea came to him when he saw one of his gardeners playing with his own son. He asked the gardener if his boy might like to earn some money by playing with William. The deal was struck, and William had a new playmate. His name was Martin.

Martin was under strict instructions from Sir Andrew not to do anything that might hurt William. But at the same time Sir Andrew explained that he expected William to get a bit dirty, and the odd scratch or bruise was all part of growing up. Martin's father had taken Martin aside and told him the opposite – that if William should come back with a mark on him, Martin would be in trouble.

Martin had seen William from afar and thought he was a strange elfin thing. He and some of the village boys laughed at William sometimes after church when no one was looking. William never even seemed to notice – he was always in a world of his own.

Martin was happy to take Sir Andrew's money but realised very fast that there was no way to get William to act like a normal boy. He could hardly even get him to run. Martin knew Sir Andrew wanted William climbing trees and so on, but what if he fell? It would be Martin's fault, and he'd get a thrashing.

So Martin and William would trail round the grounds, William desperate to get back to his books and Martin bored stiff. He'd never met anyone like William. Sometimes William would just come to a halt and stare ahead. Martin would ask him what the matter was, and William would tell him about a picture he was thinking of drawing or a story he'd read.

Eventually Sir Andrew saw that there had been no great transformation in William and told Martin his services would no longer be needed. Martin would miss the money, but he would not miss the chore of being with William.

"Go and tell your father to meet me at the eye-catcher," Sir Andrew told Martin, walking away.

William hadn't really been listening but suddenly took an interest when he heard this word he did not recognise. He turned to Martin and asked, "What did Papa say?"

"He wants me to fetch my father," said Martin.

"But I heard him say 'eye-catcher'," said William, frowning. "What's that?"

Martin shook his head and replied, "How can you have lived here all this time and never heard about the eye-catcher before?"

William shrugged. "I bet I know lots more things than you," he said.

"Is that right, Master William?" said Martin.

"Yes," said William. "I heard Father tell my mother that you might not know anything about mathematics or history or poetry, but at least you could throw a ball and climb a tree."

Martin scowled. He decided it was time to have some fun at William's expense. He remembered an old story his uncle had tried to frighten him with when he was small.

"Perhaps I shouldn't tell you about the eye-catcher," said Martin. "I wouldn't want to scare you."

"I'm not scared," said William. "Tell me."

"Are you sure, Master William?" said Martin.

"Yes," said William. "I insist."

Martin smiled to himself. *You insist, do you?* he thought. Martin turned to face William.

"Well, Master William," Martin said. "That tower over there is haunted."

William stared at Martin and then out of the window towards the tower. Martin had to stop himself from laughing.

"You mean there's a ghost there?" said William nervously. "Truly?"

"More of a demon really, Master William," said Martin, enjoying himself. "They call it an eye-catcher because it catches the eyes of anyone who looks at it. They say that if you see this demon, it's the last thing you ever see."

William had already begun to wish he had not insisted on hearing the story.

"But how does it catch your eyes?" William asked, his voice wobbling with the effort of trying not to sound frightened.

"I'm not sure this is the kind of thing for such young ears, Master William," said Martin. He shook his head and started to walk away.

"Tell me!" cried William. "You have to. Or I shall tell Father. I shall tell him you pinched me."

Martin turned slowly round.

"Very well, Master William," he said. "As you insist, I can't refuse. They say that the eye-catcher has these long fingernails ..."

Martin held up his hands like claws and left William to imagine the long fingernails they might be tipped with. Martin made scratching motions in the air. William took a step back and looked towards the tower.

"But why would my father allow such a creature to live here on the grounds?" said William.

"What can he do?" said Martin. "There's no man round here who'd ever try to kill that thing. No, you have to let a demon like that be. To try to kill the eye-catcher would just make matters worse. Anyone knows that. You're too young to understand."

"No, I'm not," said William.

"You look rather scared," said Martin. "If I'm being honest."

"I'm not," said William. "Well, maybe a tiny bit."

Martin smiled and said, "You'll be scared when the eye-catcher comes to get you."

"It's not going to come," said William. "I don't believe you. It's not – is it?"

"I don't know," said Martin, shaking his head. "I hope not."

William looked away towards the tower in a panic.

"Why would it come to get me?" William asked. "What have I done?"

Martin shrugged.

"Who knows how these things work, Master William," said Martin.

"Why hasn't it come for you?" said William.

This was a good point. Martin thought for a moment.

"Because the eye-catcher comes for people who say they don't believe in it," said Martin. "I believe, you see. But I'm not supposed to talk about it. That's one of the rules. I'm taking a risk telling you, Master William. You need to believe too. And then you might be safe."

"Might?" said William.

"Probably," said Martin. "If you believe."

"I do," said William. "I do believe."

Martin smiled. "You can't just say you believe, you know," he said. "The eye-catcher knows if you're lying."

"I'm not lying," said William.

"Good," said Martin. "That's all right then. If you're sure."

Martin knew that William was not entirely sure. How could he be? William wasn't stupid. He would always have some doubt, and that would make William nervous. Martin enjoyed watching William being tormented by this over the next few days.

William found it hard to sleep and cried out in the night, getting a stern telling-off from his father. William almost mentioned the eye-catcher but remembered Martin's warning and managed to stop himself. The very fact that he and Martin had talked about it at all was dangerous and made William worry even more.

Martin saw the silly boy keep looking over his shoulder towards the tower, even though he was supposed to be trying to avoid seeing the eye-catcher. Martin found it hard to keep a straight face.

Then one day Martin was wandering aimlessly near the lake and saw William sitting at the base of a tree. His knees were pulled up to his chin, and his hands covered his eyes.

"What are you doing, Master William?" said Martin, looking past the trees towards the tower. "I'm surprised to find you so close to you-know-what."

"I wanted to sail my boat," said William.

Martin saw William's little yacht bobbing about on the lake.

"But you got scared?" said Martin.

William nodded. Suddenly Martin had stopped enjoying this prank. He was also growing concerned that William was going to forget about the secret nature of the eye-catcher and tell his father.

"Look here, Master William," said Martin. "Here's the thing. There is no eye-catcher really. Not in the way I told you. It's just an old tower and nothing else. All that other stuff was some old story my uncle used to tell me."

William shook his head but did not move his hands.

"You're trying to fool me," he said. "I know you are. You're trying to trick me into not believing, and then the eye-catcher will come for me."

"There is no eye-catcher," Martin said again. "I promise."

"It doesn't count if you just see him a bit, does it?" said William.

"What?" said Martin. "See what?"

"The eye-catcher, silly," said William. "I don't think he saw me, so I don't think it counts."

"There is no eye-catcher!" shouted Martin.

"Don't say that," said William. "Or he'll think you don't believe."

Martin breathed a great sigh of frustration. He heard an echo of his sigh and realised there was something behind him. Martin turned to find himself face to face with a huge shadowy figure. He just had time to notice the clawed hands and the long fingernails before they flew towards his face.

Martin's screams brought servants running, with Sir Andrew following behind. They found Martin flailing around on the ground. Even with all this commotion, William would not

4
4
4
4

take his hands away from his face until they were inside. He could offer no clue as to what had happened to Martin.

Sir Andrew was persuaded that it must have been some terrible accident where Martin had run into the branches of a tree – something the terrified William must have witnessed. Martin was drugged and taken to a hospital. His ravaged eyes were bandaged, but Martin never recovered.

William wanted to tell his father what had really happened by the lake, but he decided against it. He did not want to attract the attention of the eye-catcher ...

Jake and all the children looked towards the tower and the woods where Martin had been found. Jake squinted, peering out. What was that moving about among the trees? It was a boy. There was something the matter with his face. But then he was gone, disappearing behind a shrub.

The other children hadn't seemed to notice a thing, and Jake followed them as they walked behind Mrs Fox down a corridor. Jake saw the floor was puddled with water – the cleaner couldn't have mopped up properly. Mrs Fox went into a nearby room with a grand piano in the centre of it.

"This is the music room here at Grimstone Hall, as you may have guessed," Mrs Fox told them.

One of the children near the piano accidentally pressed one of the keys. It made a *plink* noise and everyone giggled.

"Let me tell you about our fifth ghost," Mrs Fox continued. "The Grimstone Hall Trust was very pleased when they managed to track down the piano that had been in this room in the 1890s. But as soon as it arrived, strange things began to happen. The piano tuner said that the piano started to play itself as he left the room. Then there were reports of sightings of a girl sitting at the piano ..."

ghost 5

Grimstone Hall had a new lease of life in the twentieth century. It was the place to be in the 1920s. It had been bought by the very wealthy Lady Violet Godwin, who was friend to the rich and famous. The weekend parties here were well known, and everyone who was anyone longed for an invitation.

Lady Violet's daughter, Margaret, was always asked to play the piano for the guests who came to stay. It had become something of a tradition for the family. But it was a tradition that had overstayed its welcome – like some of the guests at Grimstone Hall.

When Margaret had been younger, her piano playing and singing had been charming. The applause she got from listeners was genuine. It had been sweet. Margaret's habit of biting the tip of her tongue as she played had been endearing.

But the years had rolled by, and Margaret's playing never reached the level her mother had hoped for. She had improved. On a good day, she had become competent. Margaret could work her way through one of the less demanding classical piano pieces, if she put her mind to it. But the effort was there for all to see – and hear – as Margaret gasped a great sigh of relief at the end.

Guests at Grimstone Hall would sometimes make jokes about Margaret's playing when they thought no one from the family was around to hear them. But most visitors just saw it as the price they had to pay for an otherwise lovely weekend.

One day, by chance, Margaret's mother happened to hear two famous actors talking about Margaret's playing. She paused by the door, waiting to feel a warm glow of pride. Instead, she felt the warm glow of embarrassment as the two actors joked about Margaret's "horribly dull" playing and "silly" singing.

The very next day, Margaret's mother told Margaret that she had hired a music teacher. He would be arriving the following week to give her piano lessons every day.

"But I don't need lessons," said Margaret.

"Nonsense," her mother replied. "Of course you do."

"I don't want lessons," insisted her daughter.

"But you need to improve," said her mother with a smile. "You want to keep your audience happy, don't you?"

"Not really," said Margaret. "I don't think I care."

"Don't care?" said her mother. "What on earth can you mean? Of course you care. We all care. Now you will stop this nonsense. A music teacher has been employed and music lessons will be given. That is an end to the matter."

Margaret let out a huge sigh, turned and walked away, stomping upstairs to her bedroom. She flung herself dramatically across her bed, scowling at the ceiling. There Margaret stayed for some time, until Cook called her down for some cake.

Margaret didn't see why she had to suffer piano lessons with some stupid old teacher just so she could put on a show for her mother's awful guests.

But the piano teacher turned out to be a remarkably handsome young student, trying to earn some money during his holidays. Margaret's opinion changed. Many famous actors had visited Grimstone Hall, but Margaret thought that Mr Davis, the piano teacher, was more handsome than any of them.

Margaret became much more interested in playing the piano. Her mother had bribed Margaret with all manner of things to get her to practise before, but now she waited in the music room for Mr Davis without needing a word of encouragement.

Margaret's playing improved immediately. The practice paid off. Mr Davis was a very patient teacher, and she felt as if she could play at the Royal Albert Hall – even if in truth her playing was never more than average.

But then everything changed. Lily arrived.

Lily was Margaret's slightly younger cousin. Lily's father had died suddenly, and Lily's mother, Margaret's aunt, had gone into a terrible grief. Margaret's mother had insisted that they come and stay at Grimstone Hall for as long as they wanted.

Margaret did not take the news well. She also did not welcome the idea that Lily might join in with her piano lessons.

"But I don't want to do music lessons with Lily," said Margaret, very unhappy at the whole idea of sharing Mr Davis.

"Don't be silly, dear," said her mother.

"I'm not being silly," said Margaret. "If Lily joins the lesson, Mr Davis will have less time for me and I shan't get any better. And it's not really fair to him, is it?"

"Nonsense, Margaret," said her mother. "I've already spoken to Mr Davis. He will have to cope with having to teach two pretty girls instead of one – we are paying him handsomely for his services, after all."

Margaret stomped her foot.

"Stop that, Margaret," said her mother. "Have some sympathy for Lily. Imagine if you lost poor Papa. The piano lessons might take Lily's mind off things for a while. And think – you can do a duet at the next concert."

Margaret's mother seemed delighted with this idea. Margaret knew there was no point in trying to change her mother's mind. She would just have to think of something else. In any case, Lily seemed like a quiet mousy thing. Margaret was sure she would be able to boss Lily about. She was good at bossing people about.

At their first lesson together, Margaret watched as Lily sat down at the piano. For a long time nothing seemed to happen, and Margaret smirked. But then Lily began to play.

Margaret's face grew pinker and pinker as she listened. Lily played beautifully. Not only that, but Margaret saw that Lily was actually very pretty.

"Oh, how wonderful," said Margaret's mother. "You see, my darlings – you can both play. Our guests will be delighted."

Margaret was furious and did a very bad job of hiding it. Her mother found her sulking in her room.

"Lily has had rather a bad time of it, dear," said Margaret's mother. "So please be kind to her, won't you? Please keep her company. It's so lovely for you to have a friend to play with."

This should have made sense. Margaret did get lonely. If it were anyone else, she would have agreed that having someone of her own age to share and play things with would have been very nice indeed.

But that person could not be Lily. It could never be Lily. Margaret wasn't exactly sure why, but she did know she hated Lily. She hated her and wanted her gone.

Margaret knew exactly what she would do. She took a pair of her mother's most expensive earrings and hid them in Lily's room. Her mother was bound to miss them and start a search for them. When they were discovered in Lily's room, she would be asked to leave and that would be that. Margaret's mother could not stand any form of theft or lying.

The plan went well to start with. Margaret's mother did miss the earrings almost immediately. But instead of launching a search of the entire house, her mother simply accused the maid who cleaned her room of stealing them. The poor girl refused to confess, and Margaret's mother told her she would be dismissed.

The music lessons became a form of torture for Margaret. They were made worse because Mr Davis went out of his way to try to make sure that Margaret was not left behind.

But it was no good. Margaret knew that Lily was so much better than she was. The compliments and encouragements Mr Davis gave to Margaret only made her feel worse.

It wasn't just the piano playing. Lily was more at ease with Mr Davis than Margaret. Lily made him laugh. Margaret would come into the music room and find them chatting as if they were old friends. Margaret felt tongue-tied when she tried to talk to Mr Davis and longed to have Lily's easy-going charm.

Things came to a head at the next weekend party, when the regular crowd of artists and actors and writers turned up at Grimstone Hall. As always, they prepared themselves for the traditional concert from Margaret.

It was late in the afternoon when Margaret's mother forced the girls to plod their way through a duet. Margaret knew Lily was playing slowly and poorly on purpose so as not to make Margaret look bad. Lily was so annoying!

Then Margaret stood in the doorway and watched as Lily played a solo she'd written with the help of Mr Davis. Guests who had been looking on politely now sat up and leaned forward, smiling to each other as they listened.

Soon Margaret could not watch any longer, and she walked away down the hall, simmering with anger. Applause broke out behind her like a great clap of thunder. Margaret knew that she would never play for her mother's guests again.

Something had to be done about Lily. But what? Lily could do no wrong as far as Margaret's mother was concerned.

Margaret wandered out into the grounds. The sun was already low in the sky, and Margaret's long shadow stretched across the lawn. She went over to the old well, rooted around in the pockets of her dress, found a coin and tossed it in.

"I wish that Lily was gone," Margaret said.

"Did you say something?" said a voice behind her.

It was Lily. The idea came to Margaret right at that moment.

"What?" said Margaret. "Just making a wish."

"A wish?" said Lily. "What was it?"

"Oh, you can't tell someone your wish," said Margaret, "or else it won't come true."

Lily nodded and said, "Perhaps you could wish you were a better piano player." She chuckled. "I'm only teasing. Sorry. Don't hate me."

Margaret smiled. It was too late for that.

"Of course I don't hate you," Margaret replied. "Do you know about the stars in the well?"

"Stars?" said Lily.

Margaret turned to lean over the edge of the well.

"If you look at the water in the bottom, you can see the stars," said Margaret.

"In the bottom of a well?" said Lily. "Why would there be stars at the bottom of a well? That's silly."

"They aren't at the bottom of the well," said Margaret. "The water is at the bottom of the well and the sky is reflected in it."

"But it's not dark yet," said Lily.

"But the stars are always there," said Margaret. "Even when you can't see them. You do know that, don't you?"

"Of course," said Lily, looking up at the sky.

"Well, then," said Margaret. "We can't see the stars because it's too bright. But the reflection down in the water is dark, you see. Because of the well. And you can see the stars even in the daytime."

"Really?" said Lily.

"Cross my heart," said Margaret.

Margaret crossed her heart with one hand and crossed her fingers behind her back with the other.

"But if you don't believe me, I don't care," Margaret added. "Don't look."

Lily stood on her tiptoes and tried to look over.

"I can't see anything," she said.

Margaret saw a crate lying nearby and dragged it over to the well.

"You're not tall enough," said Margaret. "Here, stand on this."

Lily smiled, thanked her and stepped up to look over.

"I still can't see," Lily said. Her voice echoed a bit now because her face was pointing down into the well.

"You have to lean right over," Margaret told Lily. "You won't fall. I'll hold the back of your dress."

Lily leaned forward shakily.

"You won't let go, will you?" Lily said nervously.

"No," said Margaret.

"Promise?"

"Promise."

But Margaret did let go. Lily squealed but did not fall. Margaret was forced to give her the tiniest of shoves, and then Lily tumbled head first into the well. There was a bump and a splash ... and then nothing.

Margaret moved the crate back to where she had found it and returned to the well. She took a deep breath and screamed as loudly as she could.

Lily's body was lifted up from the bottom of the well. There were terrible scenes as Lily was laid out on the grass. It was dark now, and people were carrying lanterns. Margaret felt like she was watching a painting come to life. It was beautiful in a way. Margaret cried and cried. Especially when the police asked her what had happened. Margaret was good at crying.

Lily's mother had to be given medicine to make her sleep, and Margaret's mother wasn't much better. The guests stayed to comfort her, but by midday the next day they had all gone. The police had spoken to them all and they were eager to leave. There was little chance any of those guests would ever return.

Margaret kept catching her mother looking at her. Mr Davis too. She found servants talking in hushed voices, but they always became silent when Margaret came closer. She knew they suspected her of Lily's murder, but there was no proof. Margaret could see her mother wanted to ask her straight out, but she knew her mother dreaded the answer and so could not. Mr Davis left their employment the following weekend.

Margaret was sad to see Mr Davis go, but he had been so cold to her since Lily died, it was probably for the best. Still, Margaret had not found it easy to fall asleep the night after he left. She had slept for just a few hours when she heard music drifting up through the house.

It wasn't just any music, but the short piece that Lily had written and played the night she fell into the well.

Margaret ignored it at first, but the music went on and on. It became clear to her that Mr Davis had not gone at all. He must be downstairs playing the piano with her mother beside him, waiting to see what effect it would have on Margaret.

She could hardly carry on ignoring it. That would make her seem guilty. No – she had to go downstairs and act as if she was completely confused about what on earth was going on. Margaret should probably cry as well and make them feel bad for reminding her about poor Lily.

Margaret crept downstairs towards the music room. She was in bare feet to be silent and surprise them, and she almost cried out when she realised she was standing in water.

She opened the doors to the music room, and the music grew instantly louder. She could not see Mr Davis because of the piano lid, and her mother wasn't visible either. No matter. Margaret went round to confront Mr Davis and found Lily sitting at the piano keys. Lily smiled

5
5
5
5

and water dribbled down her chin and onto her soaking-wet dress.

Margaret screamed and screamed until the whole household was awake. She confessed to everything and was taken away to an asylum – a hospital for the mentally ill. Her mother left Grimstone Hall and never returned.

"Some people have said they have heard the piano playing," said Mrs Fox. "But they've always found the music room empty when they got there. Some also say they have seen wet footprints heading from the front door to the music room."

Jake remembered the water he'd seen in the corridor. Grimstone Hall must be doing all these little tricks to try to work the children up about the ghost stories, but it was all really subtle. Too subtle. Jake wasn't sure anyone else had even noticed the tricks. No one had said anything. But then nor had he.

"Very well," said Mrs Fox. "Let's move on to the setting of our next story – the library."

They followed Mrs Fox to the library. As they were passing a window, Jake saw something bright and shining out of the corner of his eye – it was moving fast across the lawn.

"Hey!" cried Jake.

Mrs Fox turned at the sound of his voice.

"Out there!" shouted Jake. "There's a … a …"

But the lawn was empty now.

"What is it, miss?" asked one of the girls.

"Nothing," Mrs Fox said, smiling at Jake. "Let's carry on."

Jake looked back at the lawn, shaking his head. He caught up with the others as they entered the library, but it wasn't like any library Jake had ever seen before. The books were old and brown, even the spines. The only writing on any of the book covers was in tiny gold letters.

"Our story involves this room," Mrs Fox began. "However the ghost we are to hear about is most often seen outside, running across the lawn towards the lake. It is an alarming sight. If I tell you more, I'll spoil the story ..."

ghost 6

In the 1970s, Grimstone Hall had become the home of Richard "Dicky" Perry. He was a famous and very rich rock guitarist and songwriter. Richard's wife, Sandra, and his twelve-year-old son, Kingfisher, lived with him at Grimstone Hall.

Kingfisher had liked his name when he was younger, but it had become a problem as he got older. Boys began to tease him about it. When Kingfisher moved to a new boarding school, he asked his father to tell the teachers to call him Richard. After a long argument, his parents agreed.

Everything was fine for a while, until a boy called Gareth Collier found out Kingfisher's real name, and then the teasing began again. There were boys with names Kingfisher thought were far sillier than his, but it didn't make any difference. For some reason Gareth and his friends found Kingfisher's name especially hilarious.

Kingfisher tried to persuade his father to let him move schools. He didn't see why he couldn't go to a local school. What was the big deal about boarding school anyway? Kingfisher's father had been to this boarding school himself and insisted that his son should follow in his footsteps.

As Kingfisher was stuck at the school, he decided that he could at least do something about Gareth. So he stole money from other children and planted it on Gareth to get him expelled. It might have worked had Kingfisher not been seen with the money. Instead of Gareth getting expelled, Kingfisher's father was called to the school.

His father didn't stick up for Kingfisher at all. It was as if he cared more about the school than his own son. Kingfisher was suspended. When they walked to the car, Kingfisher said he didn't care and was glad to get out of the school because he hated it there. Without warning, his father turned and slapped Kingfisher – once, hard across the face. They drove home in silence, Kingfisher seething with a cold fury.

When Kingfisher's father had bought Grimstone Hall, he'd also bought the contents of the library that went with it. He'd added to it over the years with several books and a small round mirror – once owned by the famous master of the occult, Dr Syrus. The library was his father's pride and joy, and so Kingfisher decided that this was where he would have his revenge.

Because the library was so valuable, Kingfisher was told never to go in there and the door was always locked. But Kingfisher knew where the key was. He also knew his mother was too interested in the garden to notice what

Kingfisher was up to. His father was due to head out on tour with his band and as soon as he left, Kingfisher went to the library.

Each day, Kingfisher took a book from the shelves at random and ripped out the centre pages, burning them in the fire later. He knew his father almost never sat and looked at the books. It would take him years to discover they were damaged.

Every time Kingfisher tore out the pages, he remembered his father's slap. He thought ruining his father's books might make him feel better, but it didn't really. But he also didn't want to stop.

Then one day Kingfisher took down a book that seemed to be bound in snakeskin. He felt sure that it must be one of those once owned by Dr Syrus. It was the kind of weird thing his father loved. Kingfisher flicked past the pages and found it empty except for one single illustration. It was drawn in a very old-fashioned, stiff kind of style. The picture showed a boy about Kingfisher's age being attacked by dogs. They were biting his legs, his arms, even his head. And drops of blood were spurting out.

It was strange that there was nothing in this book except that one weird picture. Even stranger was the fact that the boy in the illustration looked exactly like Gareth Collier from school.

Kingfisher smiled. He quite enjoyed the idea of Gareth being attacked by a pack of dogs. He decided he'd leave that book alone and put it back on the shelf, then chose another book to damage.

A couple of days later, Kingfisher was having breakfast with his mother.

"Oh my god!" said his mother, pointing to the newspaper. "Doesn't he go to your school?"

Kingfisher leaned over to have a look. It was a news story about a freak accident in which a boy had been attacked by dogs whilst out riding his bike.

Every dog in the park had suddenly run at the boy, knocking him from the bike and mauling him. The boy died later in hospital. The police had no explanation for the sudden frenzy of the dogs, all of which had now been put down. The boy's name was Gareth Collier.

Kingfisher was startled. It had to be a coincidence, didn't it? How could it not be? How could a picture in an old book show something that hadn't even happened yet? Or make it happen?

His mother couldn't stop talking about the "poor boy and his family". Whenever she spoke to anyone on the phone, she said Gareth was a "school friend" of Kingfisher's and that he had been very upset by it.

Kingfisher was surprised at how little upset he was. He would never have wanted Gareth dead, and certainly not killed by a pack of dogs, but he wasn't going to pretend he was sad. Kingfisher had hated Gareth.

To make matters worse, Joe Fallon turned up. Fallon was a former drummer with his father's band. He acted as if he had just been passing, but he only seemed to visit when Kingfisher's father was away on tour.

"Hey there, Dishwasher," Fallon said, punching Kingfisher on the arm.

Kingfisher wandered off and left Fallon and his mother talking in the lounge.

"And the poor thing was Kingfisher's best friend," he heard his mother saying to Fallon.

Kingfisher headed off to the library to have another look at the illustration and see if it really did look like Gareth. He took the book down and flicked past the pages but couldn't find the illustration anywhere. Kingfisher was sure it had been right near the beginning, but now there was a different picture.

The new picture was of a man hanging in a tree. His head was wedged into the fork in a branch so that he was dangling there. It was obvious the man was dead, and it was also obvious it was a picture of Joe Fallon.

"What's this then?" said a voice behind Kingfisher.

He turned and saw Joe Fallon standing in the doorway to the library. He shut the book.

"Wait till I tell your dad about you going into his precious library," said Fallon with a smirk.

"Wait till I tell him you always come round when he's away," said Kingfisher.

Fallon's smirk disappeared. "I wouldn't advise that, Dishwasher," he told Kingfisher. "If you know what's good for you."

Fallon walked away, and Kingfisher was left to put the book back and lock the library up. Kingfisher thought about the picture and smiled to himself.

The next day, Kingfisher heard a shriek from his mother. He found her in the kitchen with the phone in her hand.

"What is it, Mum?" Kingfisher asked.

"It's Joe Fallon," she said. "He's dead." She shook her head and put the receiver down, slumped into a chair and started to sob.

"What happened?" asked Kingfisher.

"Some kind of accident," his mother said between sobs. "He was climbing a tree and fell. What was Joe doing climbing a tree? He hates heights!"

The news report on television said that Fallon was having lunch with friends in his garden. They described him going into a kind of trance and suddenly climbing a tree. When Fallon got to the top, he stepped off and his neck was caught in the branches.

After this news, Kingfisher found it hard to get back to the library, because his mother wanted him to sit with her all the time. She seemed so sad. Kingfisher couldn't understand what she had ever seen in Fallon.

His father cut short his tour so they could all attend Fallon's funeral. The following day, Kingfisher's father left to re-join his band. His mother said she needed to go for a walk to clear her head, and Kingfisher knew he had to have one last look at the strange snakeskin-covered book in the library. He couldn't stop himself.

The picture now showed a woman lying on a road, her legs and arms poking out in unnatural positions. Kingfisher instantly recognised his mother from the clothes she was wearing and dropped the book.

He rushed out of the house and up to the gate. A man was standing over his mother, who lay dead on the tarmac in front of his car. The man turned to Kingfisher with tears running down his face. "She just stepped out in front of me, like she was in a trance."

Kingfisher stood frozen for a moment, staring at the body of his mother. Then he turned away, rushed back to the house and to the library. He checked the picture in the book, and it showed someone in flames, flailing their arms around. The next victim!

"Stop this!" Kingfisher yelled, sobbing. "No!"

He stormed out of the library and into the lounge, where a fire was burning in the grate. He hurled the book into the flames, then stood and watched it burn. Kingfisher headed to the phone in the kitchen. Should he phone the police? The ambulance? He burst into sobs and slumped to the floor.

Suddenly Kingfisher became aware of the smell of burning. He looked back towards the lounge in case the book had fallen out of the fireplace, but he soon realised the smell was coming from his own clothes.

Flames began to spring up all over Kingfisher's body. He jumped up and tried to pat the flames out, but it didn't work. He turned on the tap and tried to throw water over himself, but it made no difference.

Kingfisher heard sirens and ran outside. The rush of air only made the flames stronger. He remembered the lake and ran straight for it. As he ran, he saw flames coming from his feet and legs. His arms too. His hands. And then, faster than he could scream out for help, Kingfisher was a human candle. Flames covered his whole body, and he could run no more.

By the time anyone could reach Kingfisher, he was burned to the bone.

*

Kingfisher's father was devastated, of course, and could not stand to be in the house. He sold it very shortly afterwards and left the country to go and live in America. Even his beloved library had become tainted in his mind. The contents were sold, and the books can now be found in various collections around the world.

"Some people smell burning," said Mrs Fox to the children. "Down on the lawn there. Some people have even seen a burning boy running from the house."

"Have you, miss?" said a girl near the front.

Mrs Fox nodded. "Yes."

She looked at Jake, and Jake couldn't hold Mrs Fox's gaze. What was going on? Why did she keep looking at him like that? There was something weird about her. He'd noticed it right from the start.

"Anyway, that seems like a suitable place to end our ghost-story tour," said Mrs Fox. "The library! I hope you've all been inspired to write some fantastically creepy stories of your own. Remember, don't just repeat one of these stories I've told you. Invent your own. Use those amazing imaginations of yours. I can't wait to read what you come up with. Now, you must all be starving and it's time for lunch, so I'll take you to the dining room. It's one of the loveliest rooms in the house."

But then Jake hesitated. Didn't Mrs Fox say at the start that there were seven ghosts? Just as he thought this, Jasmine stopped and turned back.

"But, miss?" she said.

"Yes, my dear?" said Mrs Fox.

"Didn't you say there were seven ghosts?" Jasmine said. "You've only told us about six."

Jake nodded. "Yeah," he said. "I was just thinking that myself."

"Did I say seven?" said Mrs Fox. "Silly me."

"Oh," said Jasmine.

"Don't you think it's a bit odd she said seven by mistake?" said Jake. "A bit weird. You'd think she'd know how many ghosts there were."

Jasmine didn't answer but just turned and hurried off to join the others.

"Oi!" Jake shouted after her. "Ignore me then, why don't you?!"

Jasmine disappeared through the door without turning round.

"She can't hear you, Jake," said Mrs Fox. "None of them can. Only me. You always forget, don't you?"

"What?" Jake said. "What are you talking about?"

Mrs Fox took a deep breath and sighed.

"Oh, Jake," she said. "I'm so sorry. You're the seventh ghost."

Jake called out after the children.

“They can’t hear you,” Mrs Fox told Jake. “Or see you. Most people can’t. I don’t know why I can. I’ve always been able to see—”

“I’m not a ghost!” said Jake. “That would mean I was dead, and I’m not dead. Do you think I wouldn’t know?! I’m alive. Of course I am. Stop saying that or I’ll report you. You can’t say that to people. You can’t just tell people they’re dead. Now let me go!”

Mrs Fox smiled and pointed to the door. “No one’s stopping you from leaving, Jake,” she said.

“Look, I don’t know what your problem is,” said Jake, “but I came here with everyone else. The other kids have talked to me.”

“Did they?” Mrs Fox asked him. “Think. Did they really?”

Jake frowned. Had he actually had a conversation with anyone except Mrs Fox?

"Look, I'm here just the same as them," said Jake. "I wrote a story and I—"

"But that was seven years ago," said Mrs Fox. "To the day actually."

"What?" said Jake with a laugh. "What are you on about?"

"It's true," Mrs Fox said. "I'm sorry."

"I'm going to report you," said Jake. "You're a weirdo, you are. Trying to scare kids. What sort of person does that?"

"No one is forced to come here, Jake," said Mrs Fox.

"Yeah, but they don't know about all those ... whatever they were. Actors. Special effects ..."

"Did you see anyone else notice or get upset by them?" Mrs Fox asked.

"What?" Jake said. "No. But—"

“That’s because no one saw them except you, Jake,” said Mrs Fox. “And me. I see ghosts too. Some people can and some people can’t. Ghosts can see each other sometimes too ...”

“I’m not a ghost,” said Jake. “Stop saying that or ...”

“I went to your funeral,” said Mrs Fox. “It seemed only right.”

“Shut up!” said Jake.

“I didn’t know your death had anything to do with the house at first,” Mrs Fox said. “We just thought it was a terrible accident. But then you turned up here ...”

“Stop saying that!” shouted Jake.

A man walked into the room.

“All done?” the man asked Mrs Fox. “Are they having lunch now?”

“Yes, they are,” she said.

"Hey!" Jake shouted at the man. "You have to stop her! She's crazy!"

The man smiled at Mrs Fox and walked away.

"Hey!" yelled Jake.

"He can't hear you, Jake," said Mrs Fox. "Think. Remember. Stop shutting it out. It does no good. You always remember in the end."

Jake licked his lips. He was panting now – short breaths coming thin and fast. But then Jake did remember. Like the memory was coming out of a mist. He looked at the cracked mirror in the hallway. He remembered now.

"Tell me, Jake," said Mrs Fox. "Tell me again. What happened?"

Jake paused for a moment, letting all the memories come flooding back into his head, and then he began ...

ghost 7

When they first fixed Grimstone Hall up, my mum brought me here. They were letting people from the local area in to see what they'd done with the estate, you know? I suppose they wanted us to see where all that lottery money was going, seeing as we could have done with some of it round where we live.

I felt a bit bad because I'd smashed a lot of windows in this house. We'd come down here – me and some older boys. We sneaked in through the fence and threw stones at the windows. We must have smashed fifty windows. More maybe. I was a bit wild back then.

We knew the stories about Grimstone Hall being haunted. Everyone did. But no one really believed them. I remember standing on the lawn, staring up at the house and yelling, "Come on! Come and get me!" I was trying to show the older kids that I wasn't scared. Even though I was. A bit. Then I threw one last stone, heard the smash of glass and cheered.

The ghosts didn't come, but the security guards did, so we ran as fast as we could. They didn't catch us, and we laughed all the way home. But we never went back. They put CCTV cameras in not long after.

So me and my mum came to look round the house. We hadn't been here long when I saw that mirror – it was one that makes everything look weird, you know? The glass was curving out, all rounded, and I looked like I was a long way away even though I was right next to it. I felt almost as if I was falling into the mirror, and I noticed there was a crack right across it.

This posh-looking bloke came over when he saw me and Mum looking at it. He said the mirror was very old and used to belong to a magician. He said it was supposed to be cursed. I asked him about the crack, and he told us that some kids had thrown stones through the windows. One of the stones had hit the mirror.

As soon as he said it, I knew it had been me that'd cracked it. I just knew. I even knew it was that last stone I threw. I don't know how. My mum shook her head and said how terrible it was. She also said how it was bad luck to break a mirror, so whoever had thrown the stone had better look out. The man agreed. "Especially a cursed mirror," he said. And then he and Mum laughed and started talking. I turned back to the mirror, and that's when I saw it. This other face. It was a bit like me, but it wasn't me, you know?

The face was older. And a bit crazy-looking. But not just that. I could hear him – the reflection guy – speaking. He was yelling "No! No! No!" over and over. I stepped back in shock and bumped into my mum and told her what I'd seen. But when I looked back at the mirror, there was no weird face or voice yelling. My mum and the man thought I was joking or lying or something. But I wasn't.

I couldn't get that mirror out of my head after that. The crack I knew I'd put in it. The face that wasn't mine. The curse. I told myself I'd just imagined it. Imagined I'd seen that face. And how could I know it was me who threw the stone that broke it anyway? It could have been anyone. But still, it was always there in the back of my mind. In my dreams too. And my nightmares.

Then a few years later, my English teacher had this idea that I should enter the story-writing competition. I told Mr Malik there was no way I was doing extra work and I'd never win anyway. But he was all like, "You're as good as you want to be." That's his big thing. Everyone can be as good as they want to be. Yeah, right.

Then I heard that the winners would get to go on a tour round the house – and that was a different thing altogether. I was in. I wanted to see that mirror again. I needed to see it, you know? I can't explain it. I needed to see that it was just a mirror and nothing else. No magic. No curse. No other face that shouldn't be there.

Don't get me wrong, I like writing. I'm pretty good when I put my mind to it. It's just making stuff up. I'm good at that. It was a decent story too. The story I wrote. I knew it was. Mr Malik said it was the best thing he'd seen anyone write in the whole time he'd worked at the school. He said it would be a scandal if my story wasn't chosen. A scandal. Ha. That's what he said.

He didn't need to worry though, because my story got picked. I'd never won anything before, and I was surprised at how proud I felt. I turned up on the day of the tour, and there were all these other kids looking a bit nervous. Some of them had teachers or parents with them, but I was on my own.

We all signed in at the door and got given name tags, and then we went to the hall. You welcomed us to the house and started with the tour. With all the talk of ghosts and stuff, I forgot about the mirror for a while. It wasn't until right at the end of the tour that I noticed I was standing next to the mirror. That same small mirror I'd seen when I'd been here with my mum. The crack was still there, but it didn't seem scary at all now.

A girl standing next to me saw the mirror too and asked why it was cracked. You told us that someone had thrown a stone through the window and it had hit the mirror. I felt bad all over again. Again, I just had this feeling it'd been my stone that'd cracked it.

Anyway, everyone was heading off to lunch after the tour, and for the first time I leaned in to have a proper look at the cracked mirror. The face I saw in it wasn't mine. Or it was and it wasn't. It was a much younger me, looking scared and confused. It was my face. My face when I was a kid and came here with my mum. That day I saw the other face. The older face. My face.

I shouted "No! No! No!" and everyone stared at me.

You asked me what the matter was, but what was I supposed to say? That the mirror was messing with me? I just shook my head. There were a few giggles. I looked at my feet. Anywhere but at the mirror. Everyone went home or back to their schools or wherever. Me, I just walked home.

But all the way I felt weird. Like I'd walked through a cobweb. I hurried along, hunched over. I must have looked pretty odd. I passed my aunt on the street and she called out to me, but I didn't stop. I just kept walking on. When I got to the shops, I took out my phone. I was going to text my cousin, but I noticed there was a crack in the screen. A thin crack. Diagonal. Just like in the mirror.

And while I was noticing that, a video started to play on my phone. But it couldn't have been a video, because no video existed of me standing on the lawn of Grimstone Hall – of me throwing the stone and yelling "Come on! Come and get me!"

KEEP OUT

Then the screensaver showed my face. Not like a photo. It was like it was a mirror, and it kept switching between my face and the younger me and back again – with that crack cutting across it. Slicing right through it.

I was just staring and staring when someone tapped me on the back. I turned round, not knowing who was behind me – and it turned out to be this kid I recognised.

I don't even like this kid that much, but I've never been so happy to see anyone in my life, you know? I don't know what I was expecting, but I was so freaked out by that point. He asked me if I was OK. I guess I must have looked a bit weird. I said hi but told him I had to go. I turned round and then *bang*.

Everything went black for a few seconds.

When I opened my eyes, I was standing in this hall next to the cracked mirror, and you were talking about the competition. I felt like I'd just woken from a dream that was already getting hard to remember.

Mrs Fox stood for a while, not knowing what to say. It was not the first time she had heard Jake's story, but it did not get any easier to hear. A thought suddenly occurred to Jake, and he started to walk towards a large gold-framed mirror at the bottom of the stairs.

"Don't," said Mrs Fox.

"But I want to see what I look—" Jake began.

She shook her head.

"Best you don't," said Mrs Fox.

Jake stopped.

"You were looking at your phone when it happened. You stepped out in front of a car. It knocked you into the air and through a shop window. Your face ... It was badly cut. Very badly."

Jake swallowed hard. He thought of the diagonal crack in the mirror. The way his reflection was sliced in two.

"If I look that bad, how can you stand to look at me?" said Jake.

Mrs Fox smiled. "I have bad eyesight, which is a bonus. But also I have trained myself not to be shocked. It took me a while. I've seen all the ghosts in this house, and sometimes they have a habit of simply appearing in front of me, like you. I have to deal with it. It never gets easier. I'm sorry if I've looked at you strangely."

"Aren't you scared?" Jake asked Mrs Fox.

She shook her head. "I don't feel scared any more. I just feel sad. For all you ghosts."

"What happens now?" said Jake. "Where do I go?"

"You don't go anywhere," said Mrs Fox. "Or not in the way you're thinking anyway. I believe you will keep appearing. Keep taking my tour. It's part of the curse. For breaking the mirror."

"But you don't tell my story, do you?"

Mrs Fox smiled.

"No," she replied. "It doesn't seem right somehow. With you in the audience. But it seems wrong not to include you too. I can never stop myself saying seven ghosts instead of six. Every time. But no. I think I'll let you tell your story, Jake. I'll be here to listen for as long as I'm able."

Jake didn't know what to say. He looked at the floor and shook his head. He heard the voices of the other children down the corridor. He heard the sound of a piano playing faintly in the distance. Mrs Fox looked away.

When she looked back, Jake was gone.

Our books are tested
for children and young people by
children and young people.

Thanks to everyone who consulted on
a manuscript for their time and effort in
helping us to make our books better
for our readers.